Calves roll and jump in the ocean.

 Humpback whales have very strong tails.

Humpback Whales

Written by Susan Watson

STECK-VAUGHN®
COMPANY
ELEMENTARY • SECONDARY • ADULT • LIBRARY

Humpback whales live in oceans
all over the world.

Humpback whales are born where the water is warm.

Humpback whale babies are called calves

Humpback whales have very long tongues.

Humpback whales can even sing!